Dirty Bertie

FLEAS!

For Jane, for all your scootering across
London on your moped to collect
and deliver *Bertie* bits and pieces.
A big thank you ~ D R

For Laurie, who's not as dirty as he'd
like to be ~ A M

STRIPES PUBLISHING
An imprint of Magi Publications
1 The Coda Centre, 189 Munster Road,
London SW6 6AW

A paperback original
First published in Great Britain in 2006
This edition published 2011

Characters created by David Roberts
Text copyright © Alan MacDonald, 2006
Illustrations copyright © David Roberts, 2006

ISBN: 978-1-84715-221-3

Printed and bound in China.
STP/1800/0010/0911
10 9 8 7 6 5 4 3 2 1

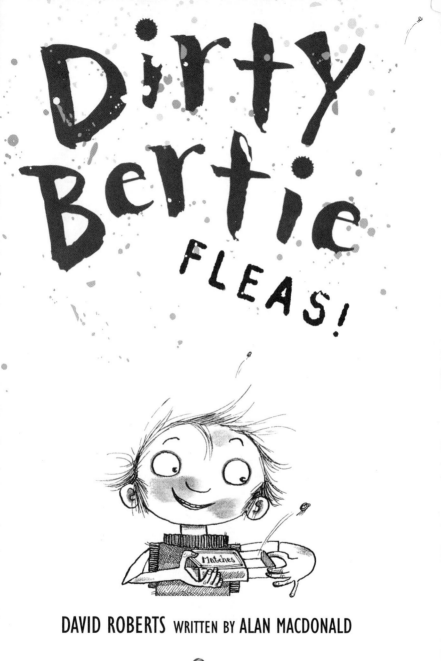

Dirty Bertie
FLEAS!

DAVID ROBERTS WRITTEN BY ALAN MACDONALD

Stripes

Contents

CHAPTER 1

SCRATCH! SCRATCH! SCRATCH!

Bertie was reading his comic at the table.

"Bertie, do you have to do that?" asked Mom.

"What?"

"Keep scratching like that. You're worse than a dog."

"I can't help it, I'm itchy," said Bertie.

Dirty Bertie

He went back to his comic.

Scratch! Scratch! He scratched his leg under the table. Scratch! Scratch! He scratched under his pajama top. Scratch! Scratch! He itched his arm.

"BERTIE! What's wrong with you?" said Mom.

"Sorry," shrugged Bertie. "I'm itchy all over."

"Let me take a look at you," said Mom. She rolled up his sleeve to inspect his arm. A look of horror appeared on her face. "Oh no! Fleas!"

"FLEAS?" cried Suzy.

"FLEAS?" cried Dad.

"Where? I can't see them!" said Bertie, peering at his arm curiously. Mom pointed at the tiny red dots above his elbow.

"There," she said. "Those are flea bites."

Suzy shifted her chair away from Bertie. "Ugh! Keep away! I don't want your fleas."

She scratched her hair. Maybe her grubby little brother had given her fleas already. Maybe she had flea bites all over her! She fled from the table and dashed upstairs to the bathroom.

"But where did he get them?" asked Dad.

"I bet I can guess," said Mom, grimly.

Dirty Bertie

Whiffer was in the living room, dozing peacefully in an armchair. Scratch! Scratch! Scratch! His back leg swished like a windshield wiper.

"There!" said Mom. "Just as I thought. There's the fleabag."

Bertie bent over to take a closer look. It was true. Whiffer's fur was alive with tiny black creatures hopping around like … well, like fleas.

Dirty Bertie

"Good grief!" said Mom. "He's crawling with them!"

"Wow! Millions!" said Bertie.

"Enough to start a flea circus," muttered Dad, keeping his distance.

"What's a flea circus?" asked Bertie.

"Oh you used to get them years ago," said Dad. "Performing fleas—doing tricks and things."

Bertie could hardly believe his ears. A flea circus! With performing fleas! What a fantastic idea! He'd already tried to train his pet earthworm, but Mom had put a stop to that when she found Arthur in his bed. But fleas? That was a much better idea. Fleas could jump and hop, so surely they could be trained to do other things? Like acrobatics. Fleas turning somersaults.

Fleas standing on each other's shoulders. Fleas flying through the air on a flea trapeze! All he had to do was catch some of Whiffer's fleas and he could have his very own circus.

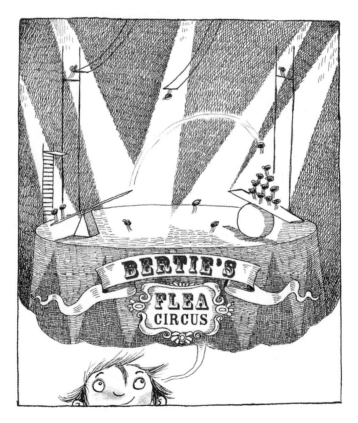

Dirty Bertie

Mom had Whiffer by the collar and was pulling him out of the armchair.

"We've got to do something," she said. "Fleas spread. They lay their eggs everywhere. They're probably all over the furniture by now!"

Just thinking about it made Dad feel itchy. "How do you get rid of them?" he asked.

Mom dragged Whiffer through the kitchen and out of the back door.

"You can buy flea shampoo—but someone will have to bath him."

"I'll do it!" said Bertie.

"NO!" said both his parents at once.

"He'll have to go to the vet's," said Mom, eyeing Dad. "You can take him."

"Why me?" said Dad. "I took him last time!"

Dirty Bertie

Dad remembered their last visit all too well. The vet had tried to force a pill down Whiffer's throat. Whiffer had spat it out three times.

"Well I can't do it," said Mom flatly. "I'm taking Suzy shopping this morning."

"But I've got work to do!" protested Dad.

"This is an emergency," said Mom. "The house is crawling with fleas. Bertie's already been bitten. They won't just walk out of the door, you know."

"All right, all right," groaned Dad. "I'll take him."

CHAPTER 2

Bertie waited till Mom and Suzy had gone out. He crept out of the back door, armed with his flea collecting kit. Whiffer wagged his tail, pleased to see him.

Bertie crouched beside him with a toothbrush and a match-box. With a little coaxing he managed to get a few of the fleas onto the end of the toothbrush.

Dirty Bertie

He shook them into the match-box and slid the lid shut quickly.

"BERTIE!" called Dad from indoors. "Can you come here a minute?"

Bertie stuffed the match-box into his pocket and went inside.

Dad was working at the computer in the back room.

"Bertie," he said. "Are you busy right now?"

"Not especially," said Bertie.

"I was thinking. Maybe you'd like to

Dirty Bertie

take Whiffer to the vet's? He's your dog."

"No thanks. Can I go now?"

"Wait!" said Dad, desperately. "I'll pay you."

Bertie paused in the doorway. "How much?"

"Two dollars."

Bertie thought about it. As usual he'd spent all his allowance.

"Three," said Dad. "Okay, five dollars— that's my last offer."

"Done!" said Bertie. He held out his hand.

"Oh no," said Dad. "You don't get paid until the job's done. And you'd better ask Gran to go with you."

Bertie nodded. Five dollars—he could do a lot with that. He was already planning what he needed for his flea circus.

Dirty Bertie

DING DONG! Bertie rang Gran's doorbell.

"Hello, Bertie!" said Gran, opening the door. "What a nice surprise. Come in!"

"I better not," said Bertie. "Dad wants me to take Whiffer to the V-E-T-S."

"The what?" said Gran.

Bertie lowered his voice. "The vet's."

"Oh, the VET'S! Why are you whispering?"

"Because I don't want Whiffer to hear. He hates the vet's."

Gran looked behind him. "Who's going with you?" she asked.

"Ah," said Bertie. "Well…"

"I see," said Gran. "I'd better get my bag then."

"So what's the matter with Whiffer?"
asked Gran, as they headed up the
street with Whiffer on his leash.

"Oh, nothing much. He's just got fleas."

"FLEAS?" Gran stopped dead.

"Yes," said Bertie. "Loads of them!
You should take a look, Gran—it's like a
flea party!"

19

Dirty Bertie

"No thanks," said Gran. "I'll take your word for it." She shook her head. "No wonder your dad didn't want to come. Typical! 'Ask your gran. She'll go to the vet's with you!'"

"Shhh!" said Bertie. "Not so loud!"

"Don't be daft, Bertie," said Gran. "He's a dog! He can't understand a word we're saying!"

The dog leash suddenly yanked her backward and they both turned around. Whiffer had stopped and was lying down on the sidewalk.

Dirty Bertie

"See?" said Bertie. "You said the word. Now we'll never get him there."

He clapped his hands. "Come on, Whiffer! Let's go!"

But Whiffer wouldn't budge. Bertie pleaded with him. He spoke in his dog training voice. He tried to drag Whiffer along by his leash, but Whiffer dug in his heels and refused to budge.

"Now what?" sighed Gran.

Bertie tried to think. If they didn't get Whiffer to the vet's there'd be no five dollar reward.

"Maggots!" he said suddenly.

"Maggots?" said Gran. "The poor dog's got fleas already! Bertie, this isn't one of your hare-brained ideas, is it?"

"No," said Bertie. "Trust me, Gran, this will work. When Dad goes fishing he uses maggots. The fish come after them. So what we need is something that Whiffer will come after!"

Gran looked at him. "Why do I get the feeling I'm going to regret this?"

"You won't," said Bertie. "I promise. Just lend me your key."

CHAPTER 3

Ten minutes later Bertie was back. Gran stared. He was wearing his helmet and roller blades, and pulling a bag that trundled along on two wheels.

"That's my shopping bag!" said Gran.

"I know," said Bertie, beaming. "It's perfect! And look what I found in the fridge!"

Dirty Bertie

He unzipped the bag to reveal a string
of sausages. "And that's my supper!" said
Gran. "What are you up to?"

"It's simple," explained Bertie. "I skate
along with the sausages in the bag. As
soon as Whiffer sees them he'll start
chasing me. He loves sausages!"

"And what am I doing while you're
zooming off with my supper?" asked
Gran.

"You hold on to Whiffer's leash," said
Bertie. "Don't let him catch the sausages
or it won't work."

Gran shook her head. "I must be mad
to listen to you."

Bertie's plan worked perfectly—at least
to begin with. Bertie whizzed off on his

roller blades with the sausages trailing from the shopping bag. As soon as Whiffer spotted them he barked and sprang to his feet. Then he was off, dragging Gran behind him at turbo speed.

"Hang on, Gran!" Bertie called over his shoulder.

"I am hanging on!" puffed Gran. "Can't you tell him to slow down?"

Bertie skated through the precinct, weaving in and out of shoppers. Whiffer bounded along behind, tugging at his leash and barking excitedly. People stopped to stare at the old lady chasing a dog who was chasing a string of sausages.

Everything might have been all right if Whiffer hadn't barked so loudly. But Whiffer always barked when he was excited and he was excited now. As they came tearing down Riddle Road, the Alsatian at Number 12 heard Whiffer barking. Seeing some escaping sausages, he eagerly joined the chase. Further down the street they met the terrier at 47 and the scruffy mongrel at 72. Both of them were fond of sausages and even fonder of a good chase.

Dirty Bertie

"Help!" cried Gran. "Bertie stop! I'm being attacked!"

Bertie looked behind him. Gran had a pack of dogs snapping at her heels. She was red in the face and skidding along like a tomato on water-skis. Whiffer was gaining on the sausages. Bertie skated faster. He could see the vet's at the end of the street.

"Hang on Gran, we're almost there!" he yelled.

Dirty Bertie

Turning sharp left, he whizzed into the drive, up a ramp and through the open door. The receptionist met him in the hall with a pile of files in her arms. Her mouth dropped open.

"I CAN'T STOP!" warned Bertie. He ploughed straight into her, scattering papers everywhere. The shopping bag did a somersault over Bertie's head and the sausages came flying out. A warm, wet tongue licked his face as Whiffer bounded on top of him.

Gran arrived soon after, panting heavily. "Well that worked a treat," she said.

CHAPTER 4

"Have they gone?" asked Bertie.

Gran glanced out of the window. "No, I'm afraid not."

They were sitting in Mr. Cage's waiting room. Outside the Alsatian and his friends kept watch by the door. They had been thrown out once but they weren't giving up that easily.

Dirty Bertie

The receptionist seemed to think it was all Bertie's fault. She said he had no business bringing every dog in the neighborhood. Bertie tried to explain they weren't his dogs but the receptionist went on telling him off. Then Gran got cross too, and said if she didn't get her a glass of water soon they'd have to call an ambulance.

At least I got Whiffer to the vet's, thought Bertie. Whiffer was sitting at his feet, happily slobbering over the sausages. It seemed to have escaped his notice that he was in a vet's waiting room. Bertie glanced around the room at the other pets. There was a parrot, a hamster, a snake curled up in a box, and a poodle that looked like a powder puff on legs.

Dirty Bertie

Scratch! Scratch! Scratch! Whiffer's
back leg was itching again.

The owner of the poodle looked
down her nose at Bertie.
"What's wrong with
your dog?"

"Oh he's fine
really," said Bertie.
"Just a few fleas."

"Fleas? I hope
you're joking?"

"No," said Bertie,
"I can show you if you
like." He reached into his pocket.
But the woman got up from her chair
and quickly backed away. She called to
her poodle.

"Fifi! Fifi, darling! Get away from that
filthy fleabag."

Dirty Bertie

"He's not a filthy fleabag!" said Bertie. "He had a bath last month."

The woman picked up her poodle and sat down on the other side of the room. Bertie and Gran were left sitting by themselves. Gran was chuckling to herself. Bertie hoped that Whiffer had managed to pass a few of his fleas to Fifi.

Just then the door to the street opened and a woman entered, carrying a fat ginger cat. Whiffer looked up and growled. Bertie noticed the door had been left open.

"'Scuse me!" he said. "You'd better shut that! There's some…"

But the warning came too late. The Alsatian and his friends had seen their chance. In a few seconds the waiting room was full of barking, yapping,

Dirty Bertie

growling dogs. The Alsatian chased the
ginger cat round a table. Whiffer and the
terrier snarled and fought over the string
of sausages. And the parrot flew over
their heads squawking, "Give us a kiss!
Give us a kiss!"

Dirty Bertie

"What's the plan now?" shouted Gran in Bertie's ear.

"I'm working on it!" replied Bertie. He tried to catch Whiffer as he ran past.

Hearing the chaos, Mr. Cage came running in and soon wished he hadn't. The cat sprang off the table and sunk its claws into his leg. Whiffer, seeing his old enemy, jumped up and knocked him to the floor. The cat and the barking dogs then chased each other round the vet in circles. Finally they escaped out the door with Whiffer leading the way.

There was a long silence as Mr. Cage sat up and stared at the wreckage of his waiting room. Bertie bent over him.

"Um, I was wondering," he asked. "Do you know anything about fleas?"

Dirty Bertie

Dirty Bertie

Dad was still working at the computer when Bertie got home.

"How did it go?" he asked, not looking up.

"Oh," replied Bertie. "It was okay, but—"

"You did get Whiffer to the vet's?" Dad interrupted.

"Oh yes, I got him there."

"And you told Mr. Cage about the fleas?"

"Yes I told him, but the thing was—"

Dad held up a hand to cut him off. "Tell me later, Bertie, I've just got to finish this." He pulled out a five-dollar bill from his wallet. "Thanks. And don't mention it to Mom, eh? It can be our secret."

Dirty Bertie

Bertie took the five-dollar bill and left. He'd tried to explain but that was the trouble with grown-ups, they never had time to listen. Anyway he had a feeling Mom and Dad would find out the truth soon enough. Perhaps when Mr. Cage phoned about the damage. Or when they noticed that Whiffer was still crawling with fleas. So it was probably best to spend the money while he had the chance.

Bertie took the match-box from his pocket and slid it open a fraction.

"Now," he said, peering inside. "Where could we buy a trapeze?"

CHAPTER 1

Bertie's class had a new teacher. Mr. Weakly was young, pale and very nervous, with round glasses that made him look like a startled owl. He was standing in for Miss Boot while she was off sick. Bertie thought she probably had a sore throat from all that shouting she did.

Dirty Bertie

He sat at the back of the class
whispering with Darren. They were
playing the Dare Game. They wouldn't
have risked anything so dangerous if Miss
Boot had been around. Miss Boot could
see you even when her back was
turned. But Mr. Weakly didn't shout or
go purple in the face like Miss Boot; he
hardly seemed to get cross at all. Darren
had already dared Bertie to burp loudly
and Bertie had dared Darren to "drop
dead" on the floor. Mr. Weakly
had merely looked up from his
book and asked
them not to be silly.

Dirty Bertie

"So?" said Bertie. "What's the dare?"

"I'm thinking," said Darren. Darren never won the Dare Game because Bertie was daring enough to do anything. Darren had once dared him to shout "Underpants!" in assembly and Bertie had yelled it at the top of his voice. But this time he was going to think of something much harder, something that even Bertie wouldn't dare to do. A smile slowly spread across his face. He had it.

"Okay," he said. "I dare you to lock Mr. Weakly in the store room."

Bertie gaped at him. "What?"

"That's the dare," said Darren. "I did mine, now it's your turn. Unless you're chickening out."

"Who says I'm chickening out?" said Bertie.

Dirty Bertie

Bertie glanced over at the store room. It was little more than a tiny cupboard which Miss Boot kept locked at all times. Bertie had been in there once to get some printer paper. It was stuffy and the light didn't work. He wondered if Mr. Weakly was scared of the dark… Still, a dare was a dare and he wasn't about to back down.

"All right," he said. "I'll do it."

Bertie's chance came a few minutes later. Mr. Weakly took off his reading glasses and asked them to copy some questions into their workbooks. Bertie raised his hand.

"Yes? What is it?" asked Mr. Weakly.

"I've run out of space in my workbook, sir," said Bertie.

Dirty Bertie

"Oh," said Mr. Weakly. "Um, what do you normally do?"

"Miss Boot keeps new workbooks in the store room," said Bertie, pointing at the door. "The key's in the drawer."

"Thank you, um…" said Mr. Weakly, forgetting Bertie's name. "The rest of you carry on with your work."

Mr. Weakly found the key and unlocked the store room door. He disappeared inside, leaving the door open and the key in the lock. Bertie could hear him rummaging on the shelves, looking for the workbooks.

"Go on!" whispered Darren. "Before he comes out!"

Bertie slid out of his seat and crept toward the door. One or two of the class looked up from their work.

Dirty Bertie

Bertie reached out a hand.

"SLAM!" The door swung shut.

"CLICK!" The key turned in the lock.

"OH!" cried Mr. Weakly from inside. "What's happening?"

Bertie pocketed the key and turned to Darren in triumph. The class were all staring at him open-mouthed.

"You've locked him in!" said Darren.

"I know," grinned Bertie. "That was the dare."

Dirty Bertie

"Yeah, but I didn't think you'd actually do it. What are you going to do now?" asked Darren.

Bertie's grin faded—he hadn't really thought that far ahead. He supposed Mr. Weakly might be a bit cross. More than a bit in fact. If he'd locked Miss Boot in the store room she would have snorted like a mad bull.

"You're for it," said Donna.

"He's going to kill you," said Know-All Nick.

"No he isn't," said Bertie. "How does he know it was me?"

CHAPTER 2

THUMP! THUMP! Mr. Weakly was knocking on the door.

"Children!" he pleaded. "Really, this isn't funny. I'm going to count to three." He counted to three. "One … two … three." Nothing happened.

Eugene looked anxious. "We can't just leave him there," he said.

Dirty Bertie

"You let him out then," said Darren. "I'm not getting into trouble."

"Why me?" said Eugene. "I didn't lock him in, Bertie did."

They all turned to look at Bertie who had crossed to Mr. Weakly's desk.

He had always wondered what it would be like to sit in the teacher's chair. He picked up Mr. Weakly's reading glasses and put them on. He added Mr. Weakly's jacket.

Dirty Bertie

"Too much chit-chat!" he said, sternly. "Get on with your work!"

"You look like a teacher," giggled Donna.

"I am a teacher," said Bertie. "I'm a very strict teacher and you'll all be staying in at recess if you don't behave!"

The class laughed. Bertie sounded like Miss Boot in a bad mood.

Dirty Bertie

He peered at them over his glasses. "Who made that pong?" he demanded. "Nick, was that you?"

The class howled with laughter. Know-All Nick turned scarlet.

"You wait. You're in so much trouble," he said. "When Miss Skinner finds out, she'll go up the wall."

Dirty Bertie

Bertie hadn't thought of Miss Skinner. The principal had a nasty habit of looking in on a class unexpectedly. If Miss Skinner found out he'd locked Mr. Weakly in the store room there'd be trouble. The thumps were getting louder. Bertie eyed the door. Maybe he should unlock it? If he moved fast he could be back in his seat before Mr. Weakly got free. He felt in his pocket. He plunged his hand in deeper. A look of horror crossed his face.

"It's gone!" he said. "I've lost the key!"

"Ha ha!" said Darren. "Come on Bertie, stop messing around."

"I'm not messing around! I put it in my pocket just now."

Bertie turned out his pocket and saw the small hole in the lining.

Dirty Bertie

The key must have slipped through and fallen out. What if he couldn't find it? What if Mr. Weakly was locked in the store room *for ever?*

"Don't just stand there!" he cried. "Help me look!"

Bertie, Darren and Donna got down on their hands and knees to search the floor.

Know-All Nick leaned back in his chair, smiling. "I told you," he jeered. "You are in *so* much trouble, Bertie."

Eugene had been keeping watch at the window. "Hurry up!" he warned. "Someone's coming!"

"What?" said Bertie.

Dirty Bertie

The class crowded at the window to look. A woman with wild red hair was striding purposefully across the yard toward them.

"Oh her," said Know-all Nick. "She's the school inspector. Miss Skinner said she was coming today."

"Inspector?" said Bertie, horrified. "What's she inspecting?"

"Our school. Weren't you listening in assembly? I expect she wants to inspect Mr. Weakly."

Dirty Bertie

They all looked at the store room door. Mr. Weakly was rattling the handle.

"We've got to get him out!" said Bertie, starting to panic.

"We?" said Know-All Nick. "You locked him in there, *you* get him out."

"But I can't find the key!" moaned Bertie.

"Do something!" cried Eugene. "She's coming up the stairs."

"Wait, I've got an idea," said Donna. "Bertie can pretend he's our teacher."

"What?" said Bertie.

"Pretend to be Mr. Weakly. You're wearing his jacket and glasses. Just say you're him."

"Are you crazy?" said Bertie. "She'll know I'm not him!"

"No she won't, she's probably never

met him. All you have to do is sit at a desk and act like a teacher. You can do it!"

"Yeah," said Darren. "I dare you!"

Bertie shot Darren a look. But maybe Donna was right. He was always doing impressions of Miss Boot, so why couldn't he be Mr. Weakly? In any case he didn't have a better idea. He sat down at the teacher's desk. The class were all out of their seats, milling around like lost sheep.

"Well SIT DOWN!" cried Bertie. "Look as if you're working!"

Everyone ran to their desks and sat down. Even Know-All Nick did as he was told. Bertie was amazed at his own power. He gave an order and everyone obeyed him. So this was what it was like to be a teacher!

CHAPTER 3

Miss Barker knocked on the classroom door and entered. She had heard scuffling as she approached but now the class all seemed to be working quietly. A scruffy boy sat at the teacher's desk in a jacket that was far too big for him.

"Good morning. My name is Miss Barker," she said. "Where is your teacher?"

Dirty Bertie

"Yes, good morning," replied Bertie. "I am the teacher."

"Don't be ridiculous!" snapped Miss Barker. "Where is Mr. Weakly?"

"Yes, Mr. Weakly. That's my name," nodded Bertie, his glasses sliding down his nose. He pushed them back up again.

Miss Barker peered down at the boy. Teachers seemed to be getting younger and younger these days, but this was absurd. This one hardly looked any older than the rest of the class. When she'd first entered the room she could have sworn he had a finger up his nose.

"How old are you?" she demanded.

"Seven … seventeen," said Bertie, correcting himself quickly.

"Seventeen? That's far too young to be a teacher!"

Dirty Bertie

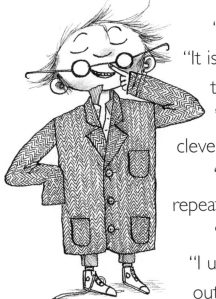

"Yes," said Bertie. "It is for a normal teacher but it's 'cos I'm more cleverer than normal."

"More cleverer?" repeated Miss Barker.

"Yes," said Bertie. "I used to get ten out of tens at school all the time. So in the end they said I just ought to get on and start teaching."

Miss Barker was about to reply but she was interrupted by a strange knocking sound.

"What's that noise?" she said.

"What noise?" asked Bertie.

"That banging noise."

Dirty Bertie

"Oh that," said Bertie. "That's just Miss Todd, teaching next door. She gets a bit cross sometimes and she starts banging on the walls and things."

"Banging on the walls? Good heavens!" said Miss Barker.

She made a note in her black file and turned back to Bertie. "Well," she said, "if you really are Mr. Weakly you better get on with the lesson."

"What?" said Bertie.

"The lesson. The lesson you're teaching."

"Oh yes, that," said Bertie. He gulped and pushed his glasses back up his nose. Miss Barker's face had gone all blurry. She seemed to be waiting for him to start. But what could he teach? He knew a lot about fleas—maybe he should draw some fleas on the board?

Dirty Bertie

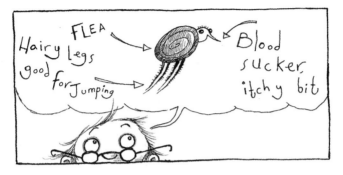

The banging from the store room started up again. He had to do something to drown out the noise.

"Math!" he said, practically shouting. "We were just going to do a few sums." The class stared at him blankly, all except Darren who was pulling faces at him from the back row.

"Darren!" said Bertie.

"Yes?"

"Stand up," said Bertie.

Darren stood up.

"What is two plus two?" asked Bertie.

Dirty Bertie

Darren thought a moment. "Four," he said.

"Very good, sit down," said Bertie. "Eugene."

"Yes, Bertie … I mean yes, sir," said Eugene, standing up.

"What are three twos, Eugene?"

"Six!" squeaked Eugene.

"Very good," said Bertie. "Nick."

Know-All Nick got to his feet. "Miss Barker—" he began, but Bertie cut him off.

"Pay attention, Nick. What is 2,740 times 7 million?"

Know-All Nick's mouth dropped open.

"Come on, come on," said Bertie, enjoying himself. "I haven't got all day!"

"I … I … don't know," stammered Know-All Nick.

Dirty Bertie

Bertie peered over his glasses. "Tut tut, Nick! Extra homework for you tonight."

CHAPTER 4

THUMP! THUMP! THUMP! The banging from the store room was deafening.

"Help!" cried Mr. Weakly. "Can anyone hear me?"

Miss Barker stood up. "There's someone behind that door!" she said.

"No um ah … I don't think so," mumbled Bertie.

Dirty Bertie

"Let me out! PLEASE!" begged Mr. Weakly.

"There is someone in there," said Miss Barker. "I can hear them shouting!"

Bertie's heart sank. Miss Barker hurried over to the store room and spoke through the door.

"Hello?"

"Hello!" replied Mr. Weakly. "Thank heavens! Who's that?"

"This is Miss Barker—the school inspector."

"Oh dear!" said Mr. Weakly in a faint voice.

"What are you doing in there?"

"I'm locked in!" said Mr. Weakly. "I came in to get a book and the door shut and now I'm locked in."

"Wait there!" said the inspector. "I'm going to fetch a teacher."

"I *am* a teacher," said Mr. Weakly. "I'm Mr. Weakly."

Miss Barker looked puzzled. "But I thought ... Mr. Weakly is right here…"

She turned back to the teacher's desk. But there was no sign of the scruffy boy she had been talking to—only a pair of glasses and a crumpled jacket that lay on his chair. Bertie had seized his chance to escape… He'd had enough of teaching for today. As he slid into his place he felt something sharp in his pocket. He pulled it out and stared at the silver key in surprise.

"Look!" he whispered to Darren. "It was in my other pocket all the time!"

Dirty Bertie

Know-All Nick had turned round in his seat. He raised his hand in the air.

"Miss Barker! Miss Barker!" he said. "Bertie's got something to show you!"

Dirty Bertie

The next day Miss Boot was back.

"Let's begin with Art," she said, with a gleam in her eye. "We'll need brushes and powder paints. Bertie, perhaps you'd like to fetch them from the store room?"

Bertie turned pale. He suddenly didn't feel well. "ME?" he said.

Dirty Bertie

FIRE!

CHAPTER 1

BOOF! Bertie landed two-footed in the big pile of leaves, scattering them everywhere.

"My go!" said Darren.

"HEY, YOU TWO! OFF THERE!" roared an angry voice. A bald, red-faced man was striding across the playground toward them.

Dirty Bertie

"Uh-oh," said Darren. It was Mr. Grouch, the school janitor.

"What do you think you're doing?" demanded Mr. Grouch.

"Um, jumping in leaves," said Bertie.

"Do you know how long it took me to sweep those up?" shouted Mr. Grouch, waving his broom.

Bertie picked up a leaf and put it back on the pile. "Sorry Mr. Grouch, we were only playing."

"Well DON'T play! Not where I'm working."

"But this is a playground."

Mr. Grouch narrowed his eyes. "Are you trying to be funny?"

"No, Mr. Grouch," replied Bertie.

"Then don't answer back. And keep out of my way!"

Dirty Bertie

Mr. Grouch glared after Bertie and Darren as they trudged off. Mr. Grouch didn't like children and he didn't like mess. Most of all he didn't like Bertie. It was Bertie who left muddy footprints all over Mr. Grouch's newly washed floors. It was Bertie who drew faces on Mr. Grouch's spotless windows.

Dirty Bertie

And Mr. Grouch was sure it was Bertie who had flooded the boys' bathroom by trying to flush away an entire roll of toilet paper. In Mr. Grouch's view, Bertie was a menace. In Bertie's view, Mr. Grouch was a vampire with a broom.

"What shall we do now?" asked Darren, as they watched the janitor sweep the leaves back into a neat pile. Bertie wasn't listening. He was staring at something coming along the street. A shiny red fire truck was slowing down and signalling left. Bertie watched with growing excitement as it turned in through the school gates.

Dirty Bertie

The fire truck halted in the parking lot in front of the school and a woman in a smart blue uniform climbed out. Bertie and Darren hurried over.

"What's happening? Is the school on fire?" asked Bertie, hopefully.

"I'm afraid not," laughed the woman. "I'm Val, what's your name?"

"Bertie. Are you a fireman?"

"Well I'm a firefighter. We're here on a

visit. Didn't Miss Skinner tell you we were coming?"

Mr. Grouch came storming over with a face like thunder. He pointed at the fire truck. "You can't leave that there! It's in my way."

Val smiled. "Sorry, Miss Skinner said to park it there."

"Did she now? We'll see about that!" said Mr. Grouch, and he stormed off muttering to himself.

"Oh, dear," said Val, pulling a face. "Am I in trouble?"

"That's nothing," said Bertie. "You should try jumping in a pile of leaves."

CHAPTER 2

Bertie could hardly believe it—a real fire crew! His school hardly ever got visitors. The last one they had was the nurse who checked them for head lice.

The fire crew stayed all morning and spoke to the whole school. Bertie learned how to dial 911 and what to do in case of a fire.

Dirty Bertie

Outside Bertie and his friends staggered around wearing helmets on their heads. They sat in the red truck and turned on the flashing light. Finally they helped the fire crew unroll a hose that stretched all the way across the playground.

"Can we turn it on?" asked Bertie.

"Sorry, Bertie, not allowed," said Val. "Only if there's a real fire."

Bertie wished he could help put out a real fire. He imagined the school crackling with flames and all the teachers at the windows crying for help. He would climb up the huge long ladder and carry them down one by one. (Miss Boot could wait till last. Come to think of it, Miss Boot could climb down by herself.)

Dirty Bertie

Dirty Bertie

At lunchtime, Bertie and his friends gazed across at the fire truck longingly. "I wish we could play on it," sighed Bertie.

"Miss Boot said we're not allowed," said Eugene.

"Well I think it's cruelty," said Bertie. "Leaving a fire truck right next to a playground and then telling us we're not allowed to play on it. It's cruelty to children."

Know-All Nick had sidled up to them unnoticed. "I bet none of you have ridden in a fire truck," he said. "I have!"

"When?" said Bertie.

"Hundreds of times," said Know-All Nick. "My uncle's a firefighter and he lets me go in it whenever I like."

"I bet he doesn't," said Bertie. "How come we've never seen you?"

Know-All Nick shrugged. "Next time I'll ask him to drive right past your house, Bertie."

Bertie snorted. Know-All Nick was always making things up. Once he told them that he'd seen the Queen waiting at the bus stop. Bertie didn't believe that and he didn't believe Nick's uncle drove a fire truck. He probably drove a mail truck.

"Anyway," said Bertie. "We don't want to go in your smelly old fire truck. We've got our own." He gripped an imaginary steering wheel and flicked an imaginary switch in front of him. "Come on!" he said.

Dirty Bertie

"WOO! WOO! WOO!" went Bertie's siren as he drove off with Darren, Donna, and Eugene hanging on behind him. Nick scowled, watching them go.

They drove the fire truck four times round the playground, stopping to put out several fires on the way. When they'd had enough they flopped down on the grass to rest.

"Oh no," groaned Darren. "He's back." Know-All Nick was running toward them, waving his arms excitedly.

"Quick!" he panted. "The school's on fire!"

"Yeah, very funny," said Bertie.

"I'm not joking," said Know-All Nick. "Look over there if you don't believe me!" He pointed to the far corner of the school. They all looked. Clouds of gray smoke rose into the sky above the roof of the hall.

"WOW!" said Bertie, getting to his feet. "It *is* on fire!"

Eugene stared open-mouthed. "What are we going to do?"

"Get the fire brigade!" said Donna. "I'll run to the staff room!"

"No!" said Know-All Nick, blocking her way. "They're not in there. I looked!"

"Then where are they?"

"I don't know!" said Nick. "Maybe they went out for sandwiches. But if we don't do something it'll be too late."

Dirty Bertie

Bertie suddenly saw things clearly. For once, Nick was right. There was no time to search for the fire crew. The school was burning down and only he—Firefighter Bertie—could save it. Soon the flames would spread and in minutes the whole school would be ablaze. Trapped inside, the teachers would be burned to a frazzle. It was up to him.

"Come on!" he said.

"Where are we going?" said Darren.

"To put out the fire, of course!"

"But isn't that dangerous?" worried Eugene. "Shouldn't we fetch Miss Boot?"

"Miss Boot's no use," said Bertie. "This is a job for professionals."

Bertie reached the fire truck first. The clouds of smoke were billowing higher. He took command, shouting orders.

Dirty Bertie

"Grab the hose! Now start pulling! Eugene, you get ready to turn it on."

"Okay!" nodded Eugene.

The orange hose began to unwind as Bertie, Darren and Donna dragged it toward the clouds of smoke. Other children came running to see what the noise was about. Eugene wished he had time to go to the bathroom. Know-All Nick sat under a tree, watching them with a knowing smile.

At last they dragged the hose round the corner of the school. The smoke wasn't coming from the hall but from the yard behind it. Clouds of smoke stung Bertie's eyes, half blinding him.

"Now, Eugene!" he shouted. "Turn it on!"

Dirty Bertie

The hose gurgled, coughed and sprang into life. A jet of water shot out with a tremendous whoosh. The hose wriggled like a snake, spraying water in every direction.

"Hold it still!" urged Bertie.

"We're trying!" said Donna. At last Bertie wrestled it under control and pointed it at the fire. With a hiss, the flames died down and fizzled out.

Dirty Bertie

"We did it!" cried Bertie. "We saved the school." But as the smoke cleared he caught sight of Mr. Grouch who had been knocked right off his feet by the first blast from the hose.

"Turn it off!" he gurgled.

Bertie stared in horror. His fire crew dropped the hose and ran. The school wasn't on fire at all. The only "fire" was Mr. Grouch's bonfire, which was now a pile of damp, smoking leaves.

Dirty Bertie

Mr. Grouch sat in a puddle with water dripping from his soggy overalls.

"You wait, you little pest!" he growled. "You just wait!"

Bertie decided it was better not to wait. He turned and ran, with the angry janitor squelching after him. He could hear Know-All Nick's shrill voice calling after him.

"Run Bertie, run! YOUR UNDERPANTS ARE ON FIRE!"

CHAPTER 3

It was all Know-All Nick's fault, thought Bertie, as he swept up the soggy leaves. Nick had tricked him just to get him in trouble. But how was he to know the school wasn't on fire? You'd think teachers would be grateful when you tried to save their lives. You'd think they'd want to thank you.

Dirty Bertie

But no—the way Miss Boot talked, anyone would think he'd tried to drown Mr. Grouch on purpose! Well next time the school could just burn down.

"Can't I stop now?" he asked. "It's almost home time."

Mr. Grouch looked at his watch. "Go on then. But don't think you're getting off lightly. Your parents will be hearing about this."

Bertie trudged home gloomily. Turning into Church Lane, he saw Pamela from his class. She was standing under a tree, gazing up at a white kitten clinging to one of the branches. It mewed pitifully.

"Poor thing!" said Pamela. "I've been calling her for ages.
I think she's scared."

Dirty Bertie

"Oh," said Bertie. "D'you want me to get her down for you?"

He eyed the kitten sternly and spoke to it in his dog training voice.

"Here girl! Down girl!" The kitten stared back at him without moving.

"I'll have to climb up," said Bertie.

Pamela looked up. "It's very high."

"Oh that's not high to me," said Bertie. "I've climbed hundreds of trees higher than that."

He took off his bag and jacket and caught hold of the lowest branch.

Luckily the tree was the kind that was made for climbing. Bertie wished there were more people to see his daring rescue.

Dirty Bertie

As he climbed higher he pictured the kitten clinging gratefully to his chest. He could see her sitting on the end of a long branch. Bertie began to inch his way along, lying flat on his stomach.

"Have you got her?" called Pamela.

"Almost!" He reached out a hand. "Here puss! Here!"

The kitten got to its feet. But instead of going to Bertie, it yawned lazily and jumped down to the branch below.

In a few swift leaps and bounds it had reached the ground. Pamela scooped it up in her arms joyfully.

Dirty Bertie

"It's okay, Bertie! I've got her!" she called. "She's all right!"

Looking down, Bertie suddenly felt *he* wasn't all right. The ground seemed a long way below—much further than he thought. In fact he wasn't sure how he was going to get down. His hands were sweating and he'd started to feel dizzy. He wrapped himself round the branch, not daring to move. Pamela's voice floated up to him.

"Bertie? What are you doing? You can come down now!"

"Um … I think you'd better call for help," said Bertie.

CHAPTER 4

An hour later Bertie sat in the passenger seat of the fire truck.

"What street did you say?" asked Val.

"Digby Drive," said Bertie.

Val nodded. "I hope you're not planning to make a habit of this," she smiled, "because next time you'll be walking home!"

Dirty Bertie

Bertie's rescue from the tree had caused quite a stir. A small crowd had gathered to watch when the fire truck arrived. A ladder was extended to Bertie with Val on top to help him down. When they were safe on the ground, everyone clapped and Bertie took a bow.

But the best part of all was that he got to ride home in the fire truck.

He looked out of the window. They were passing Cecil Street. Suddenly Bertie had a brilliant idea.

"Um, could we just turn down here?" he pointed. "It's sort of on the way, and there's someone I wanted to see."

Dirty Bertie

Know-All Nick was in the living room, watching his favorite cartoon on TV. WOOO! WOOO! WOOO! A deafening noise outside made him jump. He hurried over to the open window and looked out. He blinked. Was he dreaming?

A red fire truck was driving very slowly past his house with its lights flashing and its siren blaring. And sitting in the front seat, wearing a helmet and waving to him was Dirty Bertie. The siren stopped.

"Hi, Nick!" called Bertie. "Somebody called 911. They said to come to your house right away."

"My house?" said Nick. "Why?"

Dirty Bertie

"BECAUSE YOUR UNDERPANTS
ARE ON FIRE!" shouted Bertie.